*Little Princesses*
The Lullaby Princess

# *Little Princesses*
# The Lullaby Princess

### By Katie Chase

### Illustrated by Leighton Noyes

**Red Fox**

# Special thanks to Linda Chapman

THE LULLABY PRINCESS
A RED FOX BOOK 978 0 099 48837 8 (from January 2007)
0 099 48837 X

First published in Great Britain by Red Fox,
an imprint of Random House Children's Books

This edition published 2006

1 3 5 7 9 10 8 6 4 2

Series created by Working Partners Ltd
Copyright © Working Partners Ltd, 2006
Illustrations copyright © Leighton Noyes, 2006
Cover illustration by Nila Aye

Papers used by Random House Children's Books are natural, recyclable products
made from wood grown in sustainable forests. The manufacturing processes conform
to the environmental regulations of the country of origin.

Set in 15/21pt Bembo Schoolbook

Red Fox Books are published by Random House Children's Books,
61–63 Uxbridge Road, London W5 5SA,
a division of The Random House Group Ltd,
in Australia by Random House Australia (Pty) Ltd,
20 Alfred Street, Milsons Point, Sydney, NSW 2061, Australia,
in New Zealand by Random House New Zealand Ltd,
18 Poland Road, Glenfield, Auckland 10, New Zealand,
and in South Africa by Random House (Pty) Ltd,
Isle of Houghton, Corner Boundary Road & Carse O'Gowrie,
Houghton 2198, South Africa

THE RANDOM HOUSE GROUP Limited Reg. No. 954009
www.**kids**at**randomhouse**.co.uk

A CIP catalogue record for this book is available from the British Library.

Printed and bound in Great Britain by
Cox & Wyman Ltd, Reading, Berkshire

To Saffron Cooper,
always look out for a magic princess . . .
– *L.C.*


For Emily Brimelow,
With love
– *L.N.*

## Chapter One

Rosie sat on the floor of the castle's big bathroom rummaging through a deep cardboard box filled with smooth pebbles and pretty seashells. She began to pick out a handful of cowrie shells with glossy white sides. They were all different sizes, some so tiny they were hardly bigger than her fingernail, others large enough to cover the palm of her hand.

Her five-year-old brother, Luke, was lying on the floor next to her, stacking some large flat pebbles from the box into a pile. "Look at my tower, Rosie!" he said proudly.

As he spoke, the tower wobbled and then

collapsed with a loud crash.

Rosie grinned. "Great tower, Luke!" she teased.

Luke giggled and started to stack the pebbles up again. "Never mind," he said. "I bet I can make another one that's even higher!"

Rosie rolled the cowrie shells in her hands. She had found the cardboard box at the bottom of one of the bathroom cupboards that morning while she had been helping her mum tidy up. Mrs Campbell had said that she could make a display on the bathroom shelf using the pebbles and shells.

Lifting the largest shell to her ear, Rosie listened to the soft swirling sound of the sea. It made her think of sandy beaches and blue skies. Holidays, Rosie thought longingly, as she stood up to place the shell on the shelf.

She glanced out of the bathroom window at the grey misty mountains of the Scottish Highlands and sighed. She loved living here but right now she couldn't help thinking it would be wonderful to be on a warm, sunny beach or swimming in the sea.

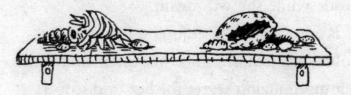

She arranged the shells on the shelf and then headed back to the old box. As she reached inside it, the sleeve of her jumper rubbed some of the dust off the top, and she saw the word *Hawaii* written in her Great-aunt Rosamund's loopy handwriting. Rosie knew that Hawaii was a tropical island far away and guessed that her adventurous great-aunt had once visited it and collected the shells and pebbles there.

I wonder where Great-aunt Rosamund is at the moment, Rosie thought. I wonder if she's near a beach right now. Her great-aunt loved visiting different countries. She was off on her travels again at the moment and had asked Rosie's family to look after her Scottish castle while she was away.

Rosie was really enjoying living in the castle, particularly since her great-aunt had left an amazing secret for her to discover. Hidden all round the castle were lots of little princesses – they might be in a picture, on a

fan, even embroidered on a rug – and when-
ever Rosie found one, if she curtseyed and
said "Hello", she was whisked off on an
amazing adventure.

I hope I find another little princess soon,
Rosie thought as she bent down to look in
the box again. She wanted a large shell
for the centre of the display now. She was
sure she could feel one, wrapped up in tissue
paper right at the bottom of the box. Rosie
pulled the package out and carefully began
to peel away the layers of thin paper. She
was right. There *was* a shell inside
the tissue paper and it was
beautiful. It was a spiral
shape with a creamy
outside and a glossy,
pale pink interior.
It was perfect for
the display.

"Rosie! Luke!" their mum called up the stairs. "Lunch time!"

"Coming!" Luke shouted eagerly. He let his pebble tower fall to the floor with another crash and ran to the door.

Rosie was about to put the shell down and follow him when she noticed something interesting. The shiny pink inside of the shell had a picture drawn in black paint on it.

She stopped and looked more closely. In the background of the drawing was a mountain that seemed to have smoke coming from the top of it. Rosie guessed that it must be a volcano. At the front of the picture, a girl was standing beside a canoe, looking anxiously at the volcano. She had long hair down to her waist, a skirt that looked like it was made of dried grass, and necklaces and anklets made of feathers and shells. On her head was a circular headdress of flowers.

She looked very beautiful, but also very sad.

Rosie's heart started to beat faster with excitement. She felt sure this was another little princess, but there was only one way to find out.

She put the shell down on the shelf and dropped into a curtsey. "Hello," she whispered, staring intently at the girl in the picture.

Immediately, a breeze seemed to blow out of the shell. It filled the bathroom with the scent of sweet flowers, pineapples and

coconuts. Rosie
gasped as the breeze
began to swirl around
her, faster and faster.
Drops of seawater
seemed to be caught
up in the air, glitter-
ing like bright
crystals. She felt
herself being lifted
up, and she gasped
and closed her
eyes; she was
going on another
adventure!

A few moments
later, Rosie felt
herself being set
gently down. There
was a smell of salt in

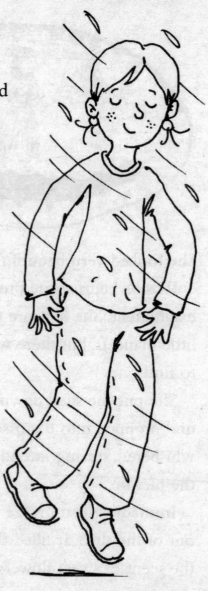

the air and a feeling of warmth on her skin.
Opening her eyes, Rosie saw that she was
now sitting in a wooden canoe on a beach
of sparkling white sand!

Rosie shifted on the seat of the canoe and
heard the crackle of dried grass as she did so.
She looked down to see that she was wearing
a grass skirt dyed a deep pinky-red colour.
A garland of yellow and white flowers hung
around her neck, and putting a hand to her
head, Rosie could feel a wreath of flowers
surrounding her red-brown curls.

Suddenly Rosie heard someone puffing in
exertion and felt the canoe move a little in
the sand. She turned round. A girl with
smooth brown skin and glossy, waist-length
dark hair was trying to push the canoe. Her
head was bent and she hadn't seen Rosie.
Rosie caught her breath in surprise.

The girl glanced up. Seeing someone

sitting in her canoe, she stopped quite still
and stared at Rosie in amazement. She was
wearing a purple grass skirt and necklaces
and anklets made of pink flowers, shells and
twinkling crystals. Over one shoulder hung
a light brown bag which had tiny, rainbow-
coloured shells sewn all over it in rows. Rosie
recognized the girl as the little princess
from the picture painted on the shell in the
bathroom.

"Who are you?" asked the astonished
princess.

## Chapter Two

Rosie stood up and stepped out of the canoe onto the white sand. "Hi, I'm Rosie," she said nervously. "I came here by magic, and I—"

"Rosie?" the princess interrupted, her dark eyes widening. "My grandmother used to tell me stories about a magic friend she had when she was younger – a girl called Rosamund who came from a faraway land. She went on adventures with my grand-mother. Do you know her?"

Rosie grinned. "I think that was my great-aunt," she explained. "Her name's Rosamund."

The princess looked eagerly at Rosie.

"Does that mean you're *my* magic friend?" she demanded.

Rosie smiled and nodded. "What's your name?" she asked.

"Kalia," the princess replied. Taking a necklace made of delicate white cowrie shells from round her own neck, she placed it over Rosie's head. "Aloha, Rosie," she said with a smile. "That's how we welcome people here to Taliki Island," she explained.

"Thank you," Rosie said delightedly, touching the delicate necklace. Her eyes fell on the canoe. "Are you about to go somewhere?"

Kalia's face fell. "Yes," she replied heavily. "I'm taking my canoe to Eppa Island. That

island over there," she added, pointing to a small hilly island that rose out of the deep sea a little way off.

"Why are you going there?" Rosie asked curiously.

Kalia looked unhappy. "Oh, Rosie. My tribe are in dreadful trouble. Pele, the goddess of the volcano on this island, has woken up and now the volcano is threatening to erupt." She turned and pointed towards the centre of the island.

Rosie looked and saw a dark peak rising out of acres of lush, green forest in the centre of Taliki Island. Clouds of black smoke were

pouring from the top of the volcano into the sky.

"If the volcano erupts, rivers of hot lava will flow down the mountain to my village," Princess Kalia went on. "Our homes will be destroyed!"

"That's awful!" Rosie exclaimed.

Princess Kalia nodded. "I can't stand by and watch that happen. I *have* to try to stop it."

"But how can you do that?" Rosie said in astonishment. "I don't think a volcano can be stopped."

"There is a legend in my tribe," Kalia explained. "It says that the Eppa people

who live
on Eppa
Island have a
magic shell
called the Shell
of Lullabies. If this
shell is brought here
and blown, the
legend says that
its pure, sweet
sound will soothe
the goddess Pele
back to sleep. And
then the volcano will

not erupt." She looked at Rosie. "I'm going to get the Shell of Lullabies and use it to calm Pele and save my village," she said determinedly. "That's why I'm going to Eppa Island."

"All by yourself?" Rosie asked, wondering

why the other people in Kalia's tribe weren't going as well.

"Yes," Kalia said, and sighed again. "No one in my tribe really believes in the Eppa people," she admitted. "They think that they are just a legend and that the Shell of Lullabies isn't real. But I *know* the Eppa exist and I'm going to find them."

"How can you be so sure they exist?" Rosie asked curiously. "Has anyone ever seen them?"

Kalia hesitated, then nodded. "*I've* seen them, Rosie," she said. "When I was little, I was on Eppa Island with my mother and some of the other villagers. They were collecting special berries for medicine, but I wandered off and got lost. I remember being in the trees, all on my own, crying, and then a group of people came. They were the same size as me but they weren't children,

they were grown-up people. They gave me
a drink of sweet guava juice and showed me
the way back to my mother."

"What did your mother say when you
told her?" Rosie asked.

Kalia bit her lip. "She didn't believe me.
She thought I imagined it all because I was
scared. But I know the Eppa are real and I
think they will help me. The trouble is, if my

mother finds out I'm going there, she'll try and stop me, so I've got to go now before anyone gets up." She started to push the canoe towards the water again.

Rosie hurried alongside her, the sand tickling her bare toes. "Can I come with you?" she asked eagerly. "We could find the Eppa people together."

Kalia looked at her in delight. "You believe me, then?"

Rosie nodded. "Yes," she said firmly. "Of course I do."

Kalia grinned. "Then what are we waiting for? Jump in the canoe and let's go!"

## Chapter Three

Rosie and Kalia pushed the wooden canoe into the sea. Kalia held the canoe steady while Rosie clambered in, and then Kalia jumped inside with her bag. There were two carved wooden paddles in the bottom of the canoe. Kalia took one and handed the other to Rosie.

"Here, you paddle this side," Kalia said, pointing to the left. "And I'll paddle on the right. You need to use your paddle like this." She showed Rosie how to sweep the paddle smoothly through the water. "You'll soon get the hang of it. Let's try."

Rosie copied Kalia's movements. Although,

at first, her paddling felt odd and jerky, she soon improved and, with Kalia paddling on one side and Rosie on the other, the little canoe was soon speeding across the waves. As the sun rose in the sky, the waves slapped against the sides of the canoe and a cooling breeze blew against Rosie's cheeks. "This is fun!" she exclaimed.

Kalia grinned. "If you think this is fun you should try catching a wave on a *paipos*," she said.

Rosie was mystified. What was a *paipos*? But before she had time to ask, Kalia spoke again.

"Look! We're almost there!" the little princess said, pointing across the sea to where Eppa Island loomed up ahead of them. Slender palm trees with glossy green leaves reached up into the sky and coconut shells littered the white sands.

As the canoe entered the shallower water near the beach, Rosie could see brightly coloured coral in the sea beneath them. White anemones waved their frond-like tentacles and striped fish darted merrily about.

"We're here!" Kalia said, as a wave swept them towards the shore. They paddled as fast

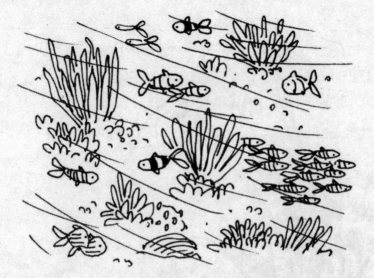

as they could onto the sand and then jumped
out. A rope was attached to the front of the
canoe and the girls used it to drag the canoe
out of the water.

Rosie looked round at the tropical island.
It seemed completely deserted. "Where do we
go?" she asked Kalia.

"I don't know," the princess admitted. "I
was just going to search until I found signs of
the Eppa people."

Just then, a yapping noise broke the silence and a fluffy white mongrel dog came bounding out of the thick vegetation around the palm trees. His stumpy tail was wagging furiously and his pink tongue was hanging out of his mouth, making him look as if he was smiling. He bounded over to the two girls.

"Hello," Rosie said, crouching down to pat him. The dog licked her hand and then bounced up to Kalia.

"Isn't he friendly?" Kalia said, stroking him. "I wonder who he belongs to."

The dog trotted away from them towards the trees. Halfway there he stopped, turned back to look at the girls, and yapped. It was almost as though he was saying, "Follow me!"

When the girls made no move to follow, he ran a few steps back towards them and barked insistently before trotting towards the trees again.

"I think he wants us to go with him," Rosie said, frowning.

Kalia nodded. "Maybe he belongs to one of the Eppa people," she said hopefully. "Come on!"

The girls ran after the dog as he bounded into the trees and onto a path that wound through the lush vegetation up towards the mountains.

Stopping every now and then to check that they were still following, the dog hurried on. After a few minutes, he gave an excited yelp and hurtled round a bend in the track. As the girls hurried round the corner after him, they saw something that made them stop in surprise.

Sitting on the track ahead of them, between the roots of an enormous palm tree, was an old woman dressed in black. She had a lined and wrinkled face, long black hair

that was streaked with grey and bright black
eyes. The dog ran up to her and put his paws
on her knees.

For a moment, Rosie wondered if this
woman was one of the Eppa people, but then
she realized that although the old lady was
quite small, she wasn't tiny enough to be one
of the Eppa.

"Hello, my dears," the old woman said, and her eyes seemed to sparkle like pieces of polished jet. "What are you doing here on Eppa Island?"

"We're looking for the Eppa people," Kalia replied. She looked at the old lady hopefully. "Do you know where we can find them?"

The old woman cackled merrily, a sound that reminded Rosie of twigs snapping and crackling in a cheerful fire. "The Eppa people! They don't exist," she declared.

But Kalia refused to be put off. "They do!" she exclaimed firmly. "I know they do. They helped me when I was little."

The old lady studied her for a moment. "I can see you still like wandering off on your own, Princess Kalia," she said thoughtfully.

"How do you know my name?" Kalia asked in surprise.

The woman laughed and nodded to herself. "That's *my* secret," she replied. Then she changed the subject. "So, tell me, Princess Kalia: why are you looking for the Eppa?"

"I want to ask them if I can borrow the Shell of Lullabies," Kalia explained.

"Kalia's tribe needs it," Rosie put in. "The volcano on Taliki Island is about to erupt."

"If I have the shell, then I can soothe the great goddess Pele back to sleep," Kalia told the old lady. "And my village will be saved."

For a second, Rosie thought she saw a mischievous smile tug at the old lady's mouth but then it was gone. "Well, maybe the Eppa do exist, and, then again, maybe they don't," the old lady said. "This island has many secrets, but only those who look hard enough will discover them. Now"– her tone changed and became more brisk– "my legs are tired. Would you two girls be kind enough to help me to the top of the hill? I'm a frail old woman and my bones don't carry me as well as they used to." She groaned and rubbed her knees as she spoke.

"Of course we'll help," Kalia said.

Rosie nodded. They did need to find the Eppa people, but they couldn't leave the old lady to struggle up the hill on her own. Rosie looked up at the mountain and wondered how they could help her to the top. "Maybe we could put our arms round

you and you could lean your weight on us,"
she suggested.

"We could try," the old lady cackled.

Rosie and Kalia put their arms around
her and began to help her up the mountain.
But the old lady was much heavier than
she looked.

"Be careful!" she exclaimed as the girls stumbled under her weight.

"Sorry!" Rosie gasped.

Kalia tripped over the old lady's foot.

"Ow!" the woman cried.

Kalia stopped. "We're never going to get to the top of the mountain like this," she sighed.

Rosie bit her lip thoughtfully. "I know. Why don't we use the canoe?" she suggested. She turned to the old woman. "You could sit in it and we could pull you up the mountainside," she said. "Would that be all right? It might be a bit bumpy, but you wouldn't have to walk at all."

The old lady nodded. "Let's give it a try," she said.

"That's a great idea!" Kalia declared. "Let's go and get the canoe."

The two girls ran back to the beach together.

The canoe was lying on the sand. "It'll be easier if we take these off," Kalia said, starting to detach two panels that hung off the sides of the canoe, looking rather like wings.

"What are they?" Rosie asked curiously as Kalia removed the first one.

"*Paiposes.* My people use them for riding over the waves," Kalia replied.

"Sort of like surfboards?" Rosie suggested, looking at the *paiposes*.

"Surfboard," Kalia repeated, trying out the word.

"Yes. That's what we call *paiposes* where I come from," Rosie explained.

She helped Kalia stick the two boards in the sand and then they used the rope to pull the canoe up the hillside to where the old lady was waiting.

"I thought you were never coming back!"

the old
woman said
impatiently as
they pulled the
canoe towards her.
"Hurry up! I haven't got
all day!"

Rosie was a bit taken aback. She
thought the old woman might have been a
bit more grateful for the lift.

"Sorry," Kalia apologized, winking at Rosie.
The two girls held the canoe steady while
their passenger clambered inside and settled
herself in a queenly way. She patted the seat
beside her and the little white dog jumped
in and sat down expectantly. The woman
chuckled, kissed his nose and then looked
up at the girls.

"Well, go on, pull!" she commanded.

Rosie and Kalia began to heave on the rope.

It was slow going, because the hillside was steep and they had to drag the canoe over clumps of grass.

"Can't you go any faster?" the old woman said huffily.

"We're pulling as hard as we can," panted Rosie. She could feel herself getting hot. It was hard work pulling the canoe and the sun was now high in the sky, its rays beating down on them.

"Come on," the old lady urged. "I'm not that heavy. After all, I'm just a little old lady!" Rosie was sure she heard the woman cackle to herself, but when she looked over her shoulder the woman just stared back at her with round black eyes and an inno-cent expression on her face.

They had just reached a thicket of trees near the top of the hill when the woman stood up. "Stop! Stop!" she cried.

The girls slowed to a halt. They were both red in the face now and breathing hard.

The old woman waved a hand airily. "I will walk from here. I have things to do!"

Before the girls knew what was happening, she had jumped lightly out of the canoe and set off into the trees, the little white dog at her heels. Rosie blinked. The old woman suddenly looked very sprightly!

"Wait!" Kalia panted.

But the old lady ignored her. She walked on swiftly, the dog bounding along behind her.

Rosie looked at Kalia. "I think there's more to this little old lady than meets the eye. Maybe she knows something about the Eppa. Come on, let's follow her!"

Kalia nodded and the two girls began to run into the trees, dragging the canoe behind them. However, no matter how fast they went, they just couldn't seem to catch up with the old woman. She looked as if she was walking fairly slowly, and yet she seemed to be covering about twice as much ground as the girls as she made her way through the trees.

"Hurry!" Rosie called to Kalia as the old woman headed out of the thicket.

"Let's leave the canoe here," Kalia suggested.

They quickly flipped it upside down so that it wouldn't slide away down the mountainside and then scrambled after the

old woman.
They dashed
out of the trees
and stopped.

They found
themselves stand-
ing at the very top
of the mountain.
From here they could
see out over the palm
trees to the beautiful
sandy beach and the azure
sea beyond, but there was no
one else anywhere in sight.
The old woman and her dog
had completely disappeared!

## Chapter Four

"Where's she gone?" Kalia said, looking around the grassy hilltop in astonishment.

"I don't know," Rosie replied, mystified. She stepped forwards, looking for the little old lady, and suddenly her foot struck something bony.

"Ouch!" exclaimed a small voice.

Rosie jumped and looked around wildly, but there was no one there.

A tiny giggle tinkled through the air.

"Ssh!" another voice hissed near Rosie's knees.

Rosie froze. "Kalia," she whispered. "Did you hear that?"

Kalia nodded, her eyes wide.

Excitement bubbled through Rosie. "Do you think it's the Eppa people?" she breathed.

Kalia stepped forwards eagerly. "We know you're there," she said. "Please come out and talk to us."

There was silence. Then Rosie thought she heard another faint giggle, although it could have been the breeze rustling the leaves on the nearby trees.

Kalia looked round. "Will you come out so we can see you?" she begged.

The silence continued.

Kalia swallowed. "You're the Eppa people, aren't you?" she said. "People say you don't exist but I *know* that you do. I'm Princess Kalia. You helped me once when I was just a little girl. Now I need your help again. Please come out." She bit her lip and added softly, "*Please!*"

There was a pause. For a moment, Rosie thought nothing was going to happen, but then the air started to shimmer with a golden light.

Rosie grabbed Kalia's arm. "Something's happening!" she gasped.

"I know," Kalia whispered, gazing around. "Look!"

A group of small round huts had begun to appear out of thin air. They were made of pale wood with dried palm leaves on the roofs. They were only about as high as Rosie's shoulders. Glancing round, Rosie saw that a whole village was appearing around them in the shimmering golden light, a village full of very small people!

Some were preparing food, others were sitting cross-legged making necklaces out of flowers and seeds. A group of children were playing tag. They all wore colourful sarongs.

"It's the Eppa!" Kalia exclaimed, as the tribe looked curiously at her and Rosie. "I knew you were real!" she declared in delight.

Three young boys who were standing near Kalia and Rosie giggled.

"You trod on my foot!" one of them called up to Rosie.

"Sorry," Rosie apologized. "Are you OK?"

The boy nodded. "I'm fine. It was worth it just to see the shocked look on your face! It was like this . . ." He pulled his face into a horrified expression. Rosie and Kalia laughed and his friends joined in. He did look funny.

Just then there was a loud yap and the little white dog came bounding out of the trees. Immediately, the Eppa people started pointing at him and murmuring to each other.

Rosie wondered why they were all so

excited about the dog. She looked round for the old lady, but there was no sign of her. Instead, a young girl with long black hair stepped out from behind a tree.

"Hello," she said, looking at Rosie and Kalia. Her voice held the hint of a grin. "Welcome to Eppa Village."

Rosie wondered who she was. She couldn't be one of the Eppa people because she was slightly taller than Rosie. Looking round, Rosie realized that the Eppa were staring at the girl in awe and whispering excitedly amongst themselves.

"So, you are here because you want the Shell of Lullabies," the girl went on. "You need it to soothe Pele, the volcano goddess. Is that so?"

How does she know that? Rosie wondered. The old woman must have told her, she thought.

Kalia was nodding. "Who are you?" she asked.

"*That* is of no importance," replied the girl with a mysterious smile. "All that matters is that I can help you. I can give you a chance to get the shell. But I need to talk to the Eppa first to see if they will agree."

She walked rapidly towards the Eppa
people, who eagerly gathered around her
in a circle. Bending low, the girl began to
whisper to them. The Eppa nodded their
heads eagerly. After a few moments,
some of them looked over their shoulders at
Rosie and Kalia and grinned. The word
*race* began to be whispered through the
crowd.

"I wonder what's going on," Rosie said in a low voice to Kalia.

"I don't know," replied the little princess. "They sound like they're planning a race of some sort. But what's a race got to do with the magic shell?"

Rosie was just as puzzled as her friend.

Just then, the girl swung round. "It has been agreed!" she declared. She strode towards Rosie and Kalia. "If you can beat me to the bottom of the hill, then the Eppa people say you may have the Shell of Lullabies. But, if you lose, then you must agree to leave this island empty-handed and never seek the shell again." She reached them and stopped. "Do you agree?" she asked.

"Is there any other way we can win the shell?" Kalia enquired cautiously.

"No," the girl replied.

Kalia looked at Rosie. "Then I guess we'll race," she agreed.

Rosie nodded. "Yes," she said. "So where do we start from and— Hey!" She broke off with an exclamation as the girl began to run towards the trees and down the mountainside.

"No rules! The fastest to the bottom wins!" the girl called over her shoulder, with a mischievous laugh.

The Eppa people began to clap their hands. "Race! Race! Race!" they chanted.

Rosie could see the girl speeding away down the mountainside, her black hair streaming out behind her and the little white dog bounding along at her feet. She had a huge head start and she was fast.

Rosie and Kalia exchanged an anxious look.

"Quick!" Rosie urged. "We must hurry!"

## Chapter Five

Kalia began to run and Rosie was about to join her when her gaze fell on the canoe that rested by a tree. "Wait, Kalia! I've had an idea," she shouted. "The girl said there were no rules, so let's use the canoe to get down the hill. We can sit in it like a toboggan and slide down the track we made on the way up!"

Kalia's face lit up. "That's a great idea, Rosie! Come on!"

The two girls sprinted over to the canoe and turned it the right way up.

"I'll push us off," Rosie cried.

The Eppa crowded after Rosie, shouting

excitedly. As Kalia jumped inside and Rosie bent down to push the canoe, the Eppa people pressed closer.

"We'll help you!" the boy whose foot Rosie had trodden on told her. "We love races!"

Rosie smiled gratefully. "Thank you." She jumped into the canoe. The Eppa people gathered round it and started to push. As it began to slide down the hill, they ran along behind, pushing it faster and faster. Rosie grabbed onto the sides as they gathered speed.

The Eppa people cheered loudly as the canoe swept out of the clearing and into the trees. Rosie was sure that she was about to shoot out at any moment. It was very bouncy.

"We're gaining on the girl!" Rosie yelled, her heart pounding as they shot out of the

thicket. The grass beneath them was smooth now and the canoe shot down the slope towards the beach, gaining speed with every second. Petals from the flowers in Rosie's and Kalia's hair swept free, floating up into the air. The girl was still ahead of them, but the friends were definitely gaining on her.

We're going to get to the bottom first! Rosie thought in delight, as the canoe raced down the slope towards the beach. I think we're going to win!

But further down the slope, a bush loomed. It had big leaves and sharp thorns and Rosie was horrified to see that the little white dog seemed to be trapped inside it. She could hear him whining plaintively.

"Kalia, I think the dog's in trouble!" Rosie
cried out. "He must have bounded into that
thorn bush and got caught."

"You're right!" Kalia replied. "And we
can't leave him there. I know it means losing
the race, but—"

"We have to stop," Rosie agreed, finishing
Kalia's sentence for her. "He might be
hurt."

Rosie grabbed a paddle and stabbed it into the ground. The canoe spun round in a half circle, bounced across the hillside and came to rest in a mound of long grass.

The girls scrambled out and raced towards the thorn bush. Sure enough, the little dog was stuck in the middle of it.

"He doesn't look injured," Rosie said in relief, as he yelped at them eagerly, his eyes bright.

Leaning into the bush, she found that the thorns had become tangled up in his coat. She started to ease the sharp points out of his fur.

Kalia reached in to help her. "Here, I'll hold the branches back," said the princess.

The thorns scratched at the girls' faces and hands, but they ignored them, and in a few seconds the dog was free. With a grateful *woof* to both of them, he jumped out of the bush, completely unharmed.

Rosie breathed a sigh of relief and watched as the dog raced to the canoe and leaped inside, looking at the girls expectantly.

"He wants to come with us!" Rosie said with a laugh.

Kalia grinned. "Let's go then!" she replied, already running back to the canoe. She turned it to face down the mountain and jumped in. Rosie gave the canoe a huge push from behind and then leaped in too, as it went sliding over the grass.

They quickly picked up speed again. Rosie gasped and held on tightly to the little dog, so that he couldn't fall out as they raced down the mountain. It felt as if they were flying!

Peering ahead, Rosie could just make out the girl's long dark hair. She was very near the beach now. Rosie thought about how desperately Kalia's people needed the Shell of Lullabies. Oh, please, she thought, willing the little canoe to go even faster. Please let us somehow reach the beach first!

## Chapter Six

For one wonderful moment, Rosie thought
they were actually going to catch up with
the girl and sweep past her at the bottom
of the hill. But amazingly, the girl seemed
to gain extra speed. She bounded down the
last few metres of grass and reached the sand
seconds before the girls slid past her.

"Oh no!" Kalia exclaimed in dismay.

Rosie's heart sank.

The girl swung round, her cheeks flushed,
her eyes sparkling, as the canoe slid to a halt
on the beach beside her. She looked at the
girls and then her gaze fell on the dog and
a smile lit up her face.

"You won," Rosie said, feeling awful. Poor Kalia. Now she was never going to have the Shell of Lullabies.

"Yes," said Kalia sadly, her shoulders sagging. "Con—congratulations," she stammered to the girl.

The white dog jumped out of the canoe and ran over to the girl. She opened her arms and he bounded into them. Tail wagging, he licked her face and whined. The girl looked up at Rosie and Kalia, her smile broadening. "Well done."

"For what? We lost," Kalia said, looking as if she was trying very hard not to cry.

"The race, yes," the girl agreed, and putting the dog down she held her arms up above her head. "But not everything." Closing her eyes, she murmured a low chant.

Rosie stared as a ball of golden light shimmered between the girl's hands.

"What's happening?" Kalia breathed.

"Look!" Rosie whispered, as a shell-shape appeared in the middle of the circle of light.

The girl finished her song, the glow faded and a large creamy shell with a glossy pink interior appeared in her hands. Putting it to her lips, she blew into it. Sweet, soothing notes floated out across the beach.

Listening to them, Rosie felt her unhappiness at losing the race drift away.

She smiled, feeling suddenly calm and peaceful. Glancing at Kalia, she saw that her friend was smiling too.

"The Shell of Lullabies," the girl said softly. She held it out to Kalia. "Here, it is yours."

Kalia and Rosie stared at her in surprise. "But we didn't win the race!" Kalia blurted out.

"No," the girl replied. "But you showed kindness when you helped a frail old woman up the hill, and when you gave up your chance of winning the race to rescue my little dog from the thorns." She smiled and pressed the shell into Kalia's hands. "And for your kindness, the Shell of Lullabies is yours. You are a worthy keeper of it because you understand that some things in life are more important than winning races."

"It's mine?" Kalia gasped, taking the shell and looking at it in wonder.

"Yes." The girl laughed. It was a mischievous, crackly sound and Rosie suddenly realized that she had heard it before: it sounded just like the old woman's merry cackle.

Rosie stared at the girl. "Are you—?" she began.

"Who I am is not important," the girl interrupted. A golden haze began to shimmer around her. "It is time for you to return home and use the shell, Princess Kalia."

"What shall I do with it afterwards?" Kalia asked her.

"You may keep it," the girl answered. "The Eppa people do not need it here on peaceful Eppa Island. Have it, so that you can always soothe the volcano and keep your people safe."

"Thank you," Kalia gasped in delight.

Rosie looked wonderingly at the amazing girl. "Who are you?" she asked. "Please tell us."

But the girl simply smiled her mysterious smile. "Goodbye," she said, and lifting her hands, she began a low chant. The next minute she and her dog vanished amidst a shimmering golden light, leaving nothing but the echo of mischievous laughter floating along the beach.

Rosie and Kalia looked at each other in amazement.

"Who was she?" Rosie asked.

"I don't know," Kalia replied, looking across the sea to her own island, where black smoke still poured from the volcano. "But whoever she was, she gave us the shell, and we must take it back to my village as quickly as we can!" Kalia put the shell carefully in her leather bag.

"Let's get the canoe!" Rosie said.

The girls raced over to the canoe, but as they began to drag it towards the sea, Rosie noticed a big hole in the bottom of it. "Oh, no! Look!" she cried.

"We must have damaged it on the way down the mountain," Kalia sighed.

"It'll sink if we take it in the sea!" Rosie exclaimed in dismay. "Kalia, I think we're stuck on Eppa Island!"

## Chapter Seven

Kalia shook her head. "Don't worry, Rosie," she said, her eyes shining. "We'll just surf back to Taliki Island!"

"Surf?" Rosie echoed.

"Yes. On the *paiposes*, or surfboards," Kalia explained, running over to the wooden boards. "If we lie on the surfboards, we can paddle towards the island. Then, when we get close enough, we can catch the waves and ride them onto the beach. Have you surfed before, Rosie?"

"No," Rosie replied anxiously.

"Don't worry," Kalia said, handing one of the boards to her. "I'm sure you'll pick it up easily. I'll show you how to do it right here on the sand. You lie on your tummy and when you feel the wave about to catch you, you jump into a crouching position on the board and stand up. Here, watch!"

Kalia put her board down on the sand and lay on top of it. "As the wave crests behind you, you need to paddle really fast, then you'll feel the board speed up and that's when you jump. Like this . . ." In one fluid movement Kalia leaped up into a crouching position.

"Go on, you try!" she urged Rosie.

Feeling slightly silly, Rosie lay down on her board.

"Imagine it's moving . . . and now jump up!" Kalia instructed.

Rosie tried but she overbalanced and fell in a heap on the sand. "Sorry," she gasped, laughing.

Kalia laughed too. "It's OK," she said, encouragingly. "You just need to practise. Try again."

Rosie lay down on the board again and tried to focus – she didn't want to let Kalia down.

"Relax," Kalia told her.

Rosie nodded and took a deep breath to steady herself. I can do this, she thought determinedly. I know I can.

"Ready to try again?" Kalia asked.

Rosie nodded. "Yes," she said, feeling calmer. "I'm ready."

"OK," Kalia said. "Jump!"

This time, Rosie managed to jump to a crouch with only the slightest wobble.

"That's great!" Kalia exclaimed. "Now you need to stand up. Like this . . ." She got onto her own board and showed Rosie how to place her feet so that she would be able to balance.

"What happens next?" Rosie asked.

Kalia's eyes sparkled. "Well, if you put all this together and catch a wave, you'll feel like you're flying!" she said. "Come on, try jumping up again."

Rosie tried a few more times, until she could jump to her feet in one smooth movement.

"Brilliant!" Kalia exclaimed at last.

Rosie glowed with pride.

Kalia picked up her board. "We'd better get going. Come on!"

They raced to the sea and waded in. As they lay down on their boards, the warm water lapped over them. Looking down, Rosie could see shoals of tiny fish darting

beneath her. They swam between her fingers as she began to paddle with her hands.

Paddling was hard work, and Rosie's arms were just beginning to feel as if they were going to fall off, when Kalia suddenly called out, "Get ready, Rosie! A wave's coming. Start paddling fast . . . Now!"

Ignoring her aching arms, Rosie paddled for all she was worth. Suddenly, she felt her board begin to lift up under her. Her heart pounded with excitement.

"Jump!" Kalia cried, leaping into the crouching position and then standing up gracefully.

Without stopping to think, Rosie copied her friend. And the next moment, she found

herself standing, balanced on a surfboard in the middle of the ocean! As the wave crested behind her, Rosie instinctively put out her arms and flexed her knees to keep her balance. The wave swept the *paiposes* forward through the blue sea, faster and faster, sending them shooting towards the golden beach.

Splashed with sea spray and buffeted by the breeze, Rosie felt as if she was flying. "Wow!" she cried. The board shifted slightly beneath her feet, but Rosie moved with it easily. "This is *fun!*"

She and Kalia raced towards the beach in a rush of foam.

As Rosie felt the surfboard run onto the sand, she jumped off, her eyes alight with excitement. "That was fantastic!" she cried.

Kalia grinned at her. "I told you you'd like it," she said happily.

A dull angry rumbling echoed across the

beach, interrupting the girls' conversation. They both turned to look. The sky around the volcano was now thick with black smoke, and red molten lava was bubbling at the top of the volcano.

"Quick!" Kalia said urgently. "We must get to the village." Dropping her board, she began to run into the trees that fringed the beach. "This way!"

Rosie charged after her.

Kalia's village was a circle of pretty round huts just inside the forest. But the whole place was in an uproar. Children were crying, while their parents were running about frantically, shouting and collecting belongings.

A tall woman with long dark hair, many necklaces and a deep purple skirt came rushing through the crowds. "Kalia!" she gasped, sweeping the princess into a hug. "Where have you been? I've been so worried about you!"

"I'm fine," Kalia said. "Mother, this is my friend, Rosie. Rosie, this is my mother, Queen Ailani."

Queen Ailani flashed a quick smile at
Rosie, but almost immediately her smile
turned to a look of intense worry as the
volcano behind her rumbled. "Come now,
girls," she urged them. "We must leave this
place immediately. The volcano's erupting!"

Her voice cracked with sudden tears. "Soon the hot lava will reach us, and our village will be destroyed!"

## Chapter Eight

"No, Mother!" Kalia exclaimed. Opening up her satchel, she pulled out the Shell of Lullabies.

Queen Ailani's eyes widened in surprise. "A shell?"

"Not just any shell," Kalia told her. "This is the Shell of Lullabies!" Taking a deep breath, she lifted the shell to her lips and blew into it. A series of soft notes streamed out.

Almost immediately, Rosie felt an overwhelming sense of peace. Looking round, she realized that the terrified villagers had heard the music too. They were all stopping and turning to look at Kalia and the magic shell.

The music poured out, calm and soothing.
And a wave of happiness swept over Rosie.
Everything is going to be all right, she
thought happily.

The people around her began to smile and Rosie could see that the panic was leaving their faces. Putting down their belongings, they drew closer to Kalia and the shell.

Still blowing, Kalia turned towards the volcano.

Rosie followed her gaze and gasped. The smoke, which only moments ago had hung around the volcano in a thick black cloud, had now lessened and turned silvery-grey. As Rosie watched, the molten lava gradually stopped bubbling and retreated back inside the volcano.

A few last wisps of white smoke drifted away
into the blue sky. And the volcano stopped
rumbling and fell silent.

A deep, peaceful sigh seemed to echo
through the village, and only then
did Kalia lower the shell.

"The Shell of Lullabies!" Queen Ailani gasped in awe.

"Yes," Kalia said, smiling at Rosie. "Rosie and I went to Eppa Island to find it." She looked at the now-peaceful volcano. "And that's not all. The shell can stay here with us on Taliki Island for ever. We need never worry about the volcano waking up again!"

The villagers gasped in delight and began to hug each other in celebration.

"But this is wonderful!" Queen Ailani exclaimed. "So the Eppa people really exist? But how did you find them and how did you persuade them to give you the shell, Kalia?"

Kalia told her mother everything that had happened on Eppa Island, from meeting the old woman to the race with the young girl. "We didn't win the race," she finished, "but the girl said we could have the shell anyway, because we had helped the old woman and the dog. I don't know who she was but she made the Shell of Lullabies appear out of thin air!"

Queen Ailani looked thoughtful. "From what you say, I think she was the great goddess Pele herself! Pele is a playful goddess. She likes to disguise herself and appear to her people to challenge us and set us tests. Your kindness and bravery must have impressed her greatly for her to have given you the magic shell."

Kalia exchanged looks with Rosie. "It was both of us. I wouldn't have got the shell if it hadn't been for Rosie. We helped the old lady and rescued the little dog together."

Rosie smiled back at her.

Queen Ailani took Rosie's hands in hers. "Our tribe will always be grateful to you for all that you did to help, Rosie," she said, her dark brown eyes warm. "You have saved our village by bringing us the Shell of Lullabies. Thank you." She turned to the rest of the tribe in delight. "From now on, we will no longer have to live in fear of the volcano!" she announced.

The villagers whooped and cheered, and Rosie and Kalia hugged each other.

"We will celebrate with a *luau!*" Queen Ailani continued, raising her voice above the noise.

"What's a *luau*?" Rosie asked Kalia
eagerly.

"A feast!" Kalia replied as everyone began
to bustle about, talking excitedly. "A feast on
the beach!"

The next hour seemed to whiz by as all the
villagers made preparations for the *luau*.
Rosie and Kalia helped dig a huge
hole on the beach and then
watched as hot rocks
were placed
inside it.

The rocks were covered with banana leaves and then meat was placed on top and covered with more banana leaves before being left to cook.

"I've never seen food cooked like that before," Rosie said.

"It's a type of cooking called *Kalua*," Kalia explained. "The meat will taste delicious. Come on, let's go and help with the rest of the food."

The girls helped carry baskets of banana bread and fruit from the village. There were platters of sticky coconut and guava cakes, slices of fresh pineapple and mango, and bowls of sweet potatoes and rice. A group of men brought drums and rattles decorated with feathers and shells down to the beach, and began to play lively music.

Soon the feast was in full swing. People ate and danced and laughed on the white sands,

the clear, turquoise waves lapping near their feet.

"This is wonderful!" Rosie exclaimed as she twirled round and round with Kalia.

The little princess grinned at her. "I'm so glad you came to visit me today, Rosie!"

"Me too," Rosie said, remembering everything they'd done together since she'd arrived that morning: paddling a canoe, meeting the Eppa people, racing down a mountainside and, best of all, surfing back to the beach. It had been an amazing day!

"Let's get some food," Kalia said, pulling her by the hand towards the tables.

Rosie piled her plate high with fruit, bread, rice and some of the meat that had cooked under the banana leaves. "Mmmm," she sighed happily as she and Kalia sat on a soft grass mat in the shade of a palm tree. "You're right," she said, having tried some of the meat. "*Kalua* cooking is delicious!"

Kalia grinned and fetched them both glasses of fresh coconut and mango juice.

Sitting together, they drank their cool drinks and watched happily as the other villagers danced, their grass skirts swirling around them, petals floating from their garlands into the sky. Eventually the sun began to set behind the now-peaceful volcano, and the blue sky was streaked with pink and gold.

"I'm going to have to go home now," Rosie said reluctantly.

"You will come back and visit us again soon, though, won't you?" Kalia said anxiously.

Rosie smiled. "Of course." She hugged her new friend. "Goodbye, Kalia."

Almost the second the words were out of her mouth, a gentle, sweet-scented breeze picked her up and Rosie felt herself being carried into the air. Moments later, she found herself

back
in the
bathroom
of the castle.
She was
home again!
Almost immediately,
Rosie's eyes fell upon
the cream shell on the
bathroom shelf. The
drawing on it looked
slightly different. She

picked it up for a closer look, and saw that the volcano was no longer smoking and that, in the picture, Kalia was smiling now. She noticed another detail and grinned – a little white dog was now running along the sand looking very happy too!

Suddenly there was the sound of running feet on the landing outside.

Luke poked his head round the bathroom door. "Why are you still looking at that

boring old shell, Rosie?"
he demanded. "Lunch is
ready and Mum won't
let me start until you
come down. Come on!"

Rosie hid a grin. If
only Luke knew the truth!
She put the shell carefully
on the shelf, right in the
centre. "OK, I'm coming," she told him.

"I'll race you to the kitchen!" Luke
challenged.

Rosie remembered the volcano goddess's
words and smiled at him. "There are more
important things in life than winning races,
Luke," she said.

"Ha!" Luke scoffed. "You're just saying
that 'cos you're a slowcoach, Rosie!"

"Who are you calling a slowcoach?"
Rosie said indignantly. Diving forwards,

she grabbed her little brother and tickled him.

Luke squealed and wriggled. "Let me go!" he shrieked, laughing.

"OK," Rosie replied, darting over to the door and slipping through it. "Come on, slowcoach!" she shouted over her shoulder.

Luke raced after her and, laughing and shouting, they rushed helter-skelter along the corridor and downstairs to the kitchen for lunch.

**THE END**

Did you enjoy reading
about Rosie's adventure with
the Lullaby Princess?
If you did, you'll love the next
*Little Princesses*
book!

Turn over to read the first
chapter of *The Silk Princess*.

## Chapter One

"Come on, Rosie!" called Luke excitedly, as he charged through the huge wooden door into the castle. "I want *my* picture frame to be the best one in the whole class!"

Rosie grinned as she followed her younger brother inside. Luke's teacher had asked the class to find things at home that they could use to decorate a picture frame, and Luke was keen to get started.

"I bet we can find lots of stuff around the castle," Rosie said. "I'm sure Great-aunt

Rosamund will have some lovely bits and pieces you can use."

"My teacher said we should look out for all sorts of things," Luke replied. "Buttons, foil, bits of material, anything!"

"And what about sequins and sparkly glitter?" Rosie suggested.

"Great! I'll look upstairs first," Luke said eagerly, and he shot off up the wide oak staircase.

Smiling to herself, Rosie walked up the stairs and wandered down the corridor towards her great-aunt's sewing room. She gazed around. The walls were lined with shelves, which were crammed with silks, satins and velvets in every colour of the rainbow. There were baskets filled with spools of coloured thread. A large, old-fashioned sewing machine stood in one corner and a tailor's dummy in another, draped with rose-red silk.

Rosie went over to look at a basket of buttons. As she did so, a photograph next to the sewing machine caught her eye. It showed Great-aunt Rosamund sitting on an elephant! Rosie grinned.

This photo must have been taken in India, Rosie thought, remembering that her great-aunt had told her stories about her trip to India. She picked up the photo for a closer look, and her gaze fell on the frame surrounding the picture. It was made out of silk and was beautifully embroidered with threads of many different colours. In one corner of the frame was a tiny woven picture of a young girl, who was also sitting on an elephant. She had long, black hair, pinned up with a pretty hairpin, which had a tiny sparkling elephant dangling from it.

Rosie gasped. "It's another little princess!" she said to herself. "I'm sure of it!"

Shaking with excitement, Rosie sank into a low curtsey, just as her great-aunt had instructed.

"Hello!" she whispered.

Immediately, a warm breeze swept towards Rosie from the picture frame. As it lifted her gently off her feet, Rosie closed her eyes. She could smell the strong scent of jasmine and exotic spices.

A second or two later the breeze died away. Rosie could feel the sun beating down on her and hear noise all around. Quickly she opened her eyes.

She was standing in the middle of a busy, bustling market. There was a stall nearby, piled high with colourful fruit and vegetables, many of which Rosie didn't recognize. Large silver dishes of spices in red, gold, orange and green were also for sale, along with silver and gold jewellery set with sparkling gems, and heavily-embroidered bedspreads and tablecloths decorated with tiny mirrors.

People hurried through the market, bargaining with the stallholders. The men wore loose trousers and shirts, and some wore turbans, while the women were dressed in saris.

"I must be in India!" Rosie told herself. She glanced down and was delighted to see that she too wore a sari. It was made of lilac chiffon, shot through with dazzling silver threads, and she had matching silver sandals on her feet.

Rosie wondered where the little princess could be. She stared round at the stalls, but the girl from the picture frame was nowhere to be seen.

I'd better go and find her, Rosie thought. So she set off, weaving her way through the crowds of people.

After a few minutes, Rosie found herself on

the edge of the market. She was in a street of small wooden shops, lined with trees. It was quieter here, though monkeys chattered and swung through the branches overhead. Rosie frowned; she couldn't see anyone else around. Where *could* the little princess be?

At that moment a young girl with long black hair came out of one of the shops. She was carrying an apricot-coloured sari in her arms. Rosie's heart began to beat faster, because the girl looked just like the little princess!

Rosie watched the girl throw the sari into a large wooden tub of water, which stood outside the shop front. There were brown onionskins floating in the tub, and the water was a sludgy brown colour.

The girl took a stick and began stirring the sari energetically in the water. As she did so, the beautiful apricot colour started to disappear, and the material turned the same dull brown colour as the water.

Rosie was puzzled. Why would anyone want to make a beautiful apricot sari that horrible shade of brown? As she wondered about this, she spotted a washing-line strung between two nearby trees. It was hung with other brown saris, which had obviously just been dyed too.

The other girl bent lower over the tub of water, and her hair swung forward. As it did, Rosie could see a tiny elephant dangling from a hairpin.

Now she was sure that this really *was* the little princess, Rosie hurried forwards. "Hello!" she called, "I'm so glad I've found you. I'm Rosie, and you must be the little princess!"

The girl stopped stirring the water and looked up at Rosie with a puzzled smile. "What do you mean?" she asked. "*I'm* not a princess!"

Read the rest of *The Silk Princess* to find out what happens next!